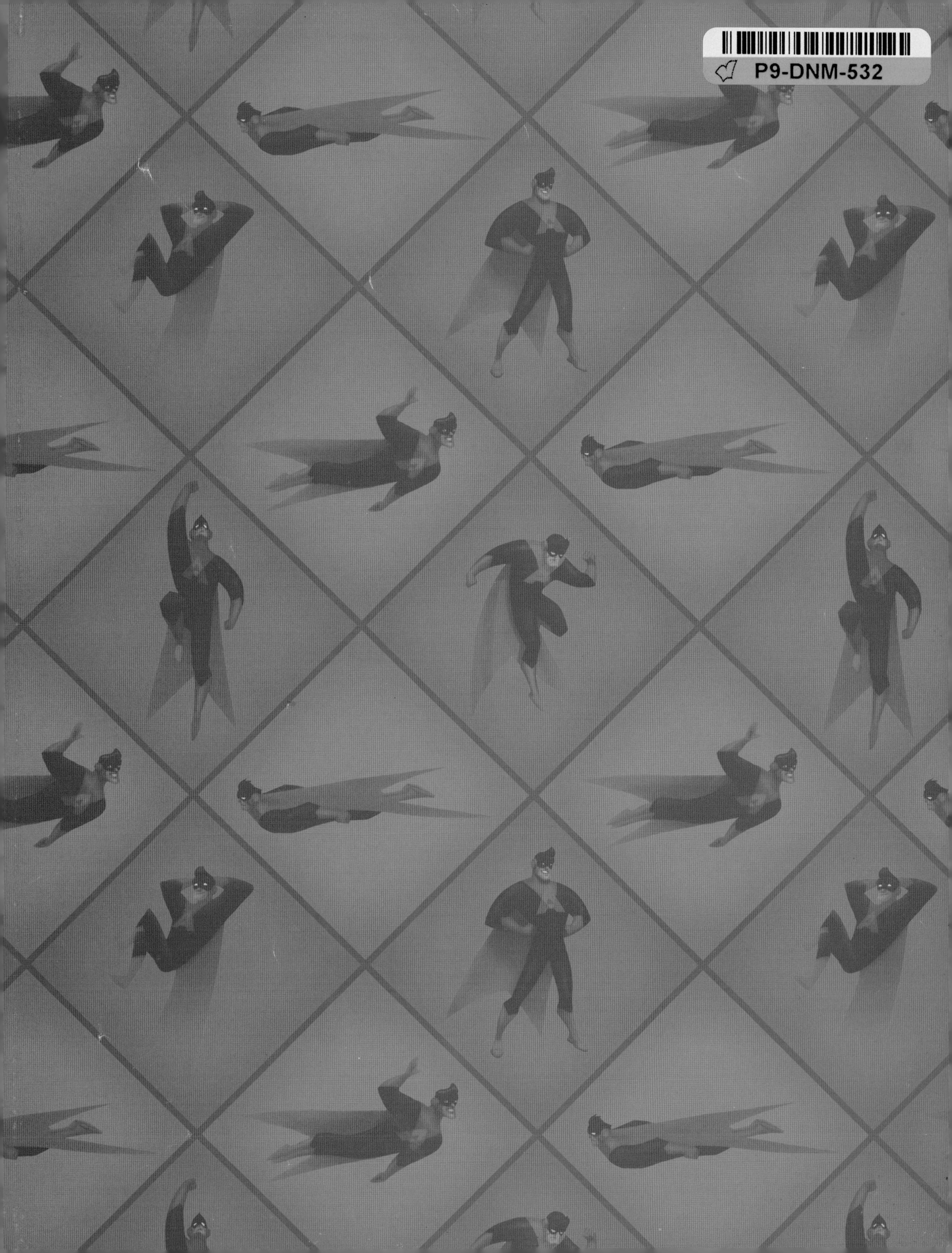

THE ASTONI

AWES

BALZER + BRAY
An Imprint of HarperCollins*Publishers*

SHING SECRET OF
OME MAN

ILLUSTRATED BY JAKE PARKER

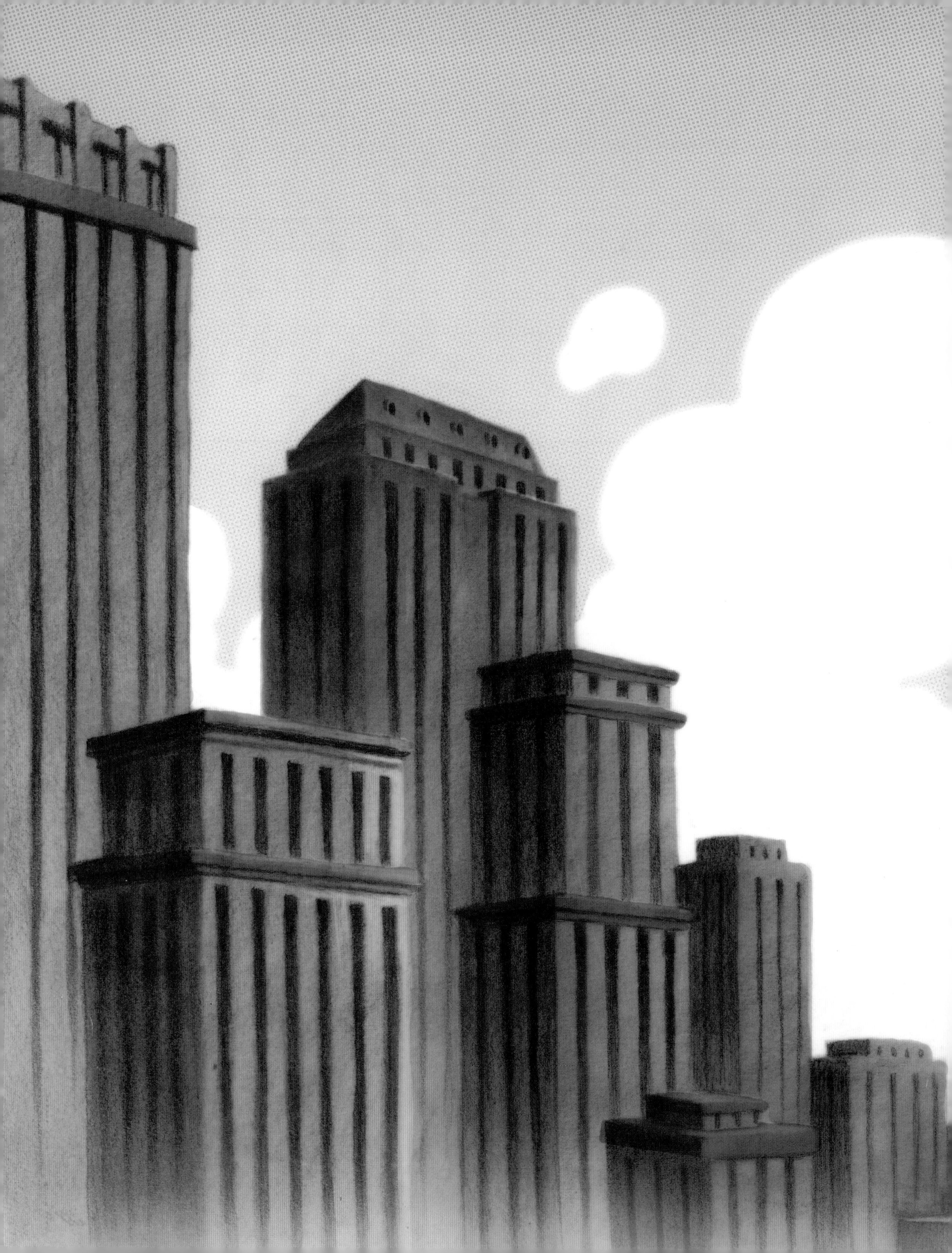

Hi! I'm a superhero. My name is Awesome Man.

I have a cape as red as a rocket,

a mask as black as midnight,

and a stylin' letter A on my chest.

I'm just basically awesome.

I can fly as high
as a satellite

and as straight
as an arrow

or through the time barrier and not get dizzy, or feel nauseous,
or smash into things . . . except on purpose. When you are a
superhero like me, sometimes you have to smash into things.

I can shoot positronic rays out of my eyeballs. And can I tell you something? Giant killer robots just hate that stuff.

You know what else is totally awesome? My trademark Awesome Power Grip. I can hug a runaway freight train. I can hug Jell-O.

SKREEECH

I can hug mutant talking Jell-O from Beyond the Stars.

But maybe the most awesome thing about me is my secret identity. Now, this is a total secret, all right? So listen closely, because I'm going to whisper it. Real low. So low that only you and Moskowitz the Awesome Dog will be able to hear me.

In real life I'm— Uh-oh!

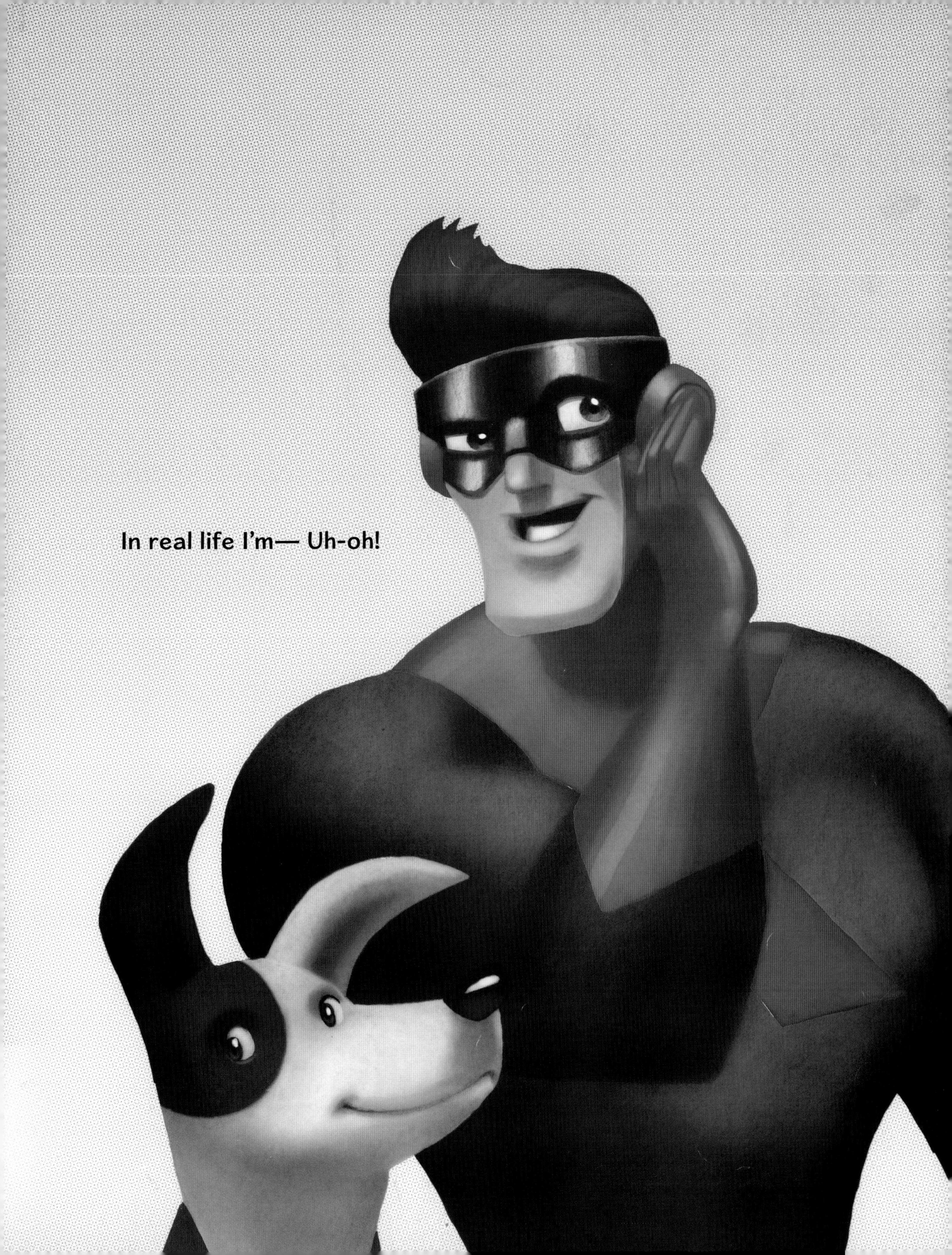

Here comes Professor Von Evil in his Antimatter Slimebot! Antimatter slime is extra gross.

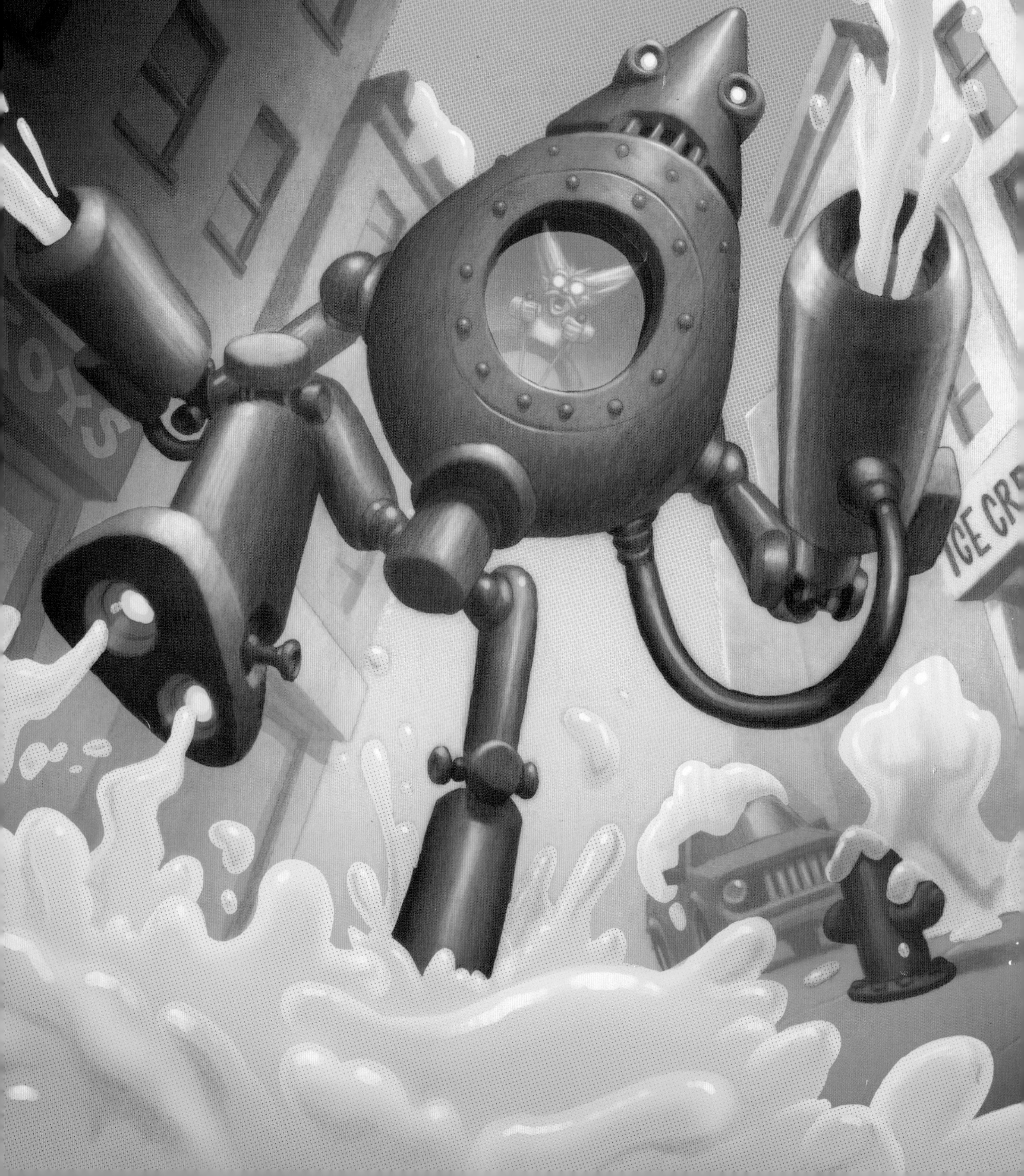

But, okay, check this out. I change into my secret identity—
and the dude just sklooshes right past me. Do you see me?
Professor Von Evil doesn't!

Then I just sneak up behind him, slap a big old power grip on his pointy head . . . and *SKA-RUNCH!* The professor gets schooled!

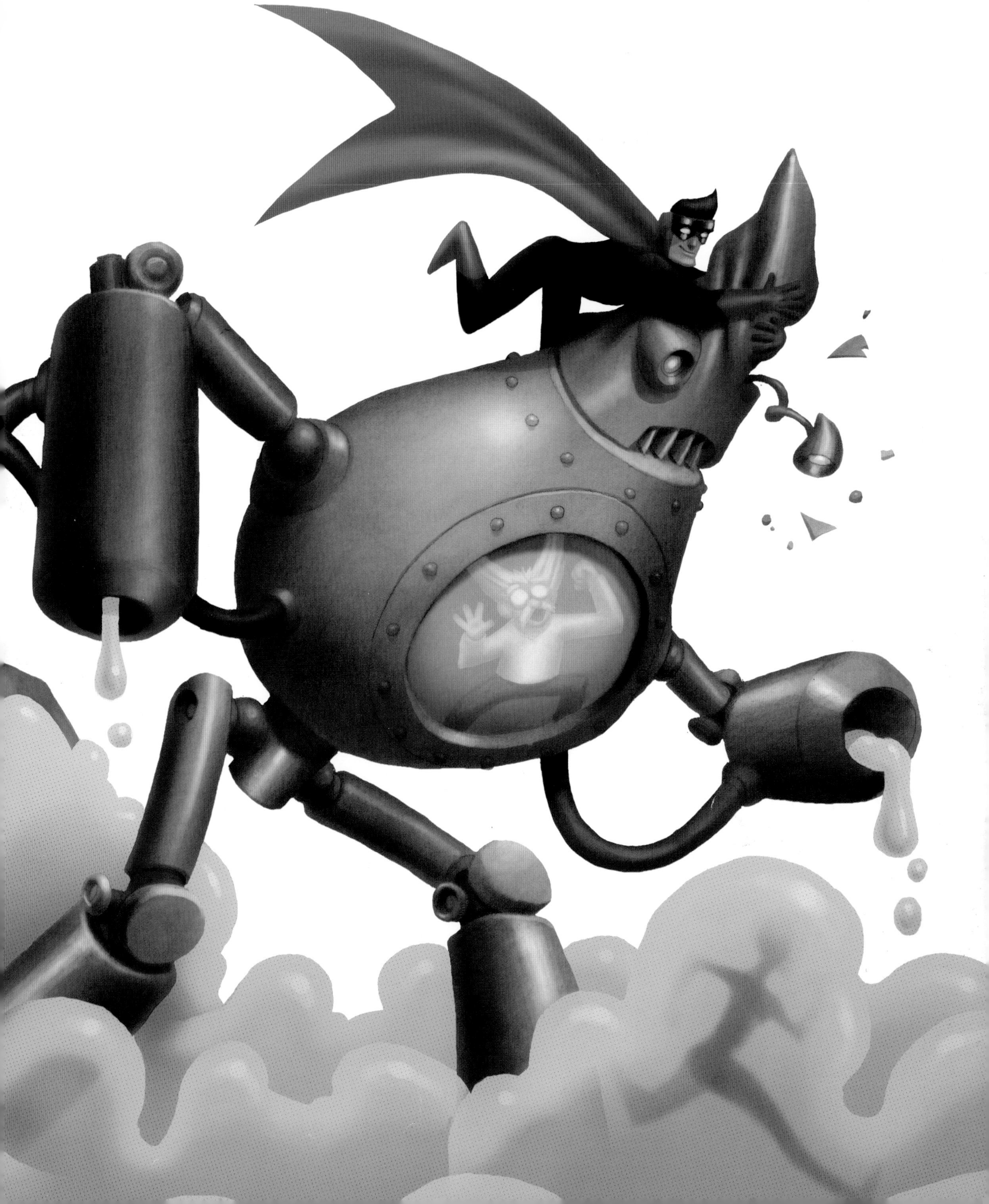

But don't think it's nonstop fun and photons being Awesome Man. Sometimes it can be a pretty hard— What the heck?

Oh man, it's the Flaming Eyeball! My arch nemesis!

I'm going to tell my mo— I mean, I'm going to use my beams to make a positronic force shield!

Shoot. The Eyeball got away. That makes me angry. And you do not want to be there when Awesome Man gets angry. It is not a pretty sight.

See, the thing is, I'm superstrong. I have to be careful.
I can't start hitting stuff or kicking stuff or throwing stuff
around, even though that's what I want to do so badly.
I might hurt somebody, or destroy a city or something.

So I fly back to the Fortress of Awesome, deep at the bottom of the deepest, darkest trench under the Arctic Ocean. It's peaceful here. Quiet and calm. I can just lie on the bed and chill for a while. I need to get a grip.

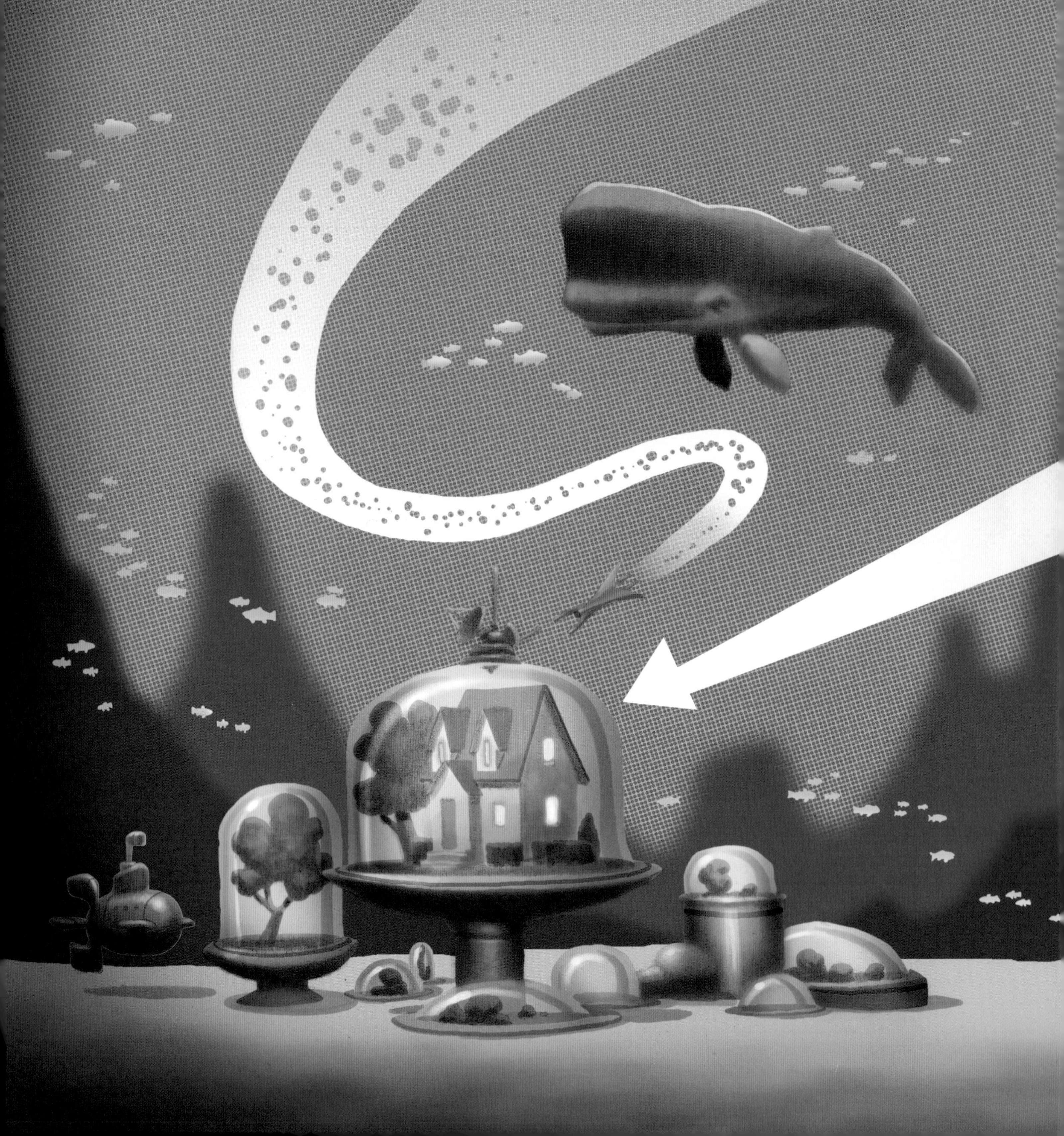

So that's what I do. I get myself in a ginormous Awesome Power Grip. It calms me right down so I can think again. And that's when I realize what my problem is: I'm almost out of positrons! All this evil-fighting can make a superhero tired. Really tired. Pooped.

(I love saying "pooped.")

The thing is, it takes a lot of energy to be Awesome Man. To be exact, it takes seven billion kilojoules per nanosecond. But sometimes I get so busy being awesome all the time . . . that I forget.

SECRET PLANS

So I call for Moskowitz on our secret frequency. She brings
me a thermovulcanized protein-delivery orb, straight from
the kitchen of the fortress. And a little packet of salt.

After I'm all calmed down and positronic again, I take off after the Flaming Eyeball. I fly west. I fly east. I fly eight times around the earth and all the way to the heart of the sun. (The Flaming Eyeball hangs out there sometimes.)

Then I see him! He goes into the hidden entrance of the Secret Headquarters of Worldwide Wickedness. I hide out there and spy on him. He's chilling with Sister Sinister and the Red Shark.

I throw an Awesome Power Grip on all three of them, give them a little blast of eye beams, kick a little bad-guy behind.

BLAST!

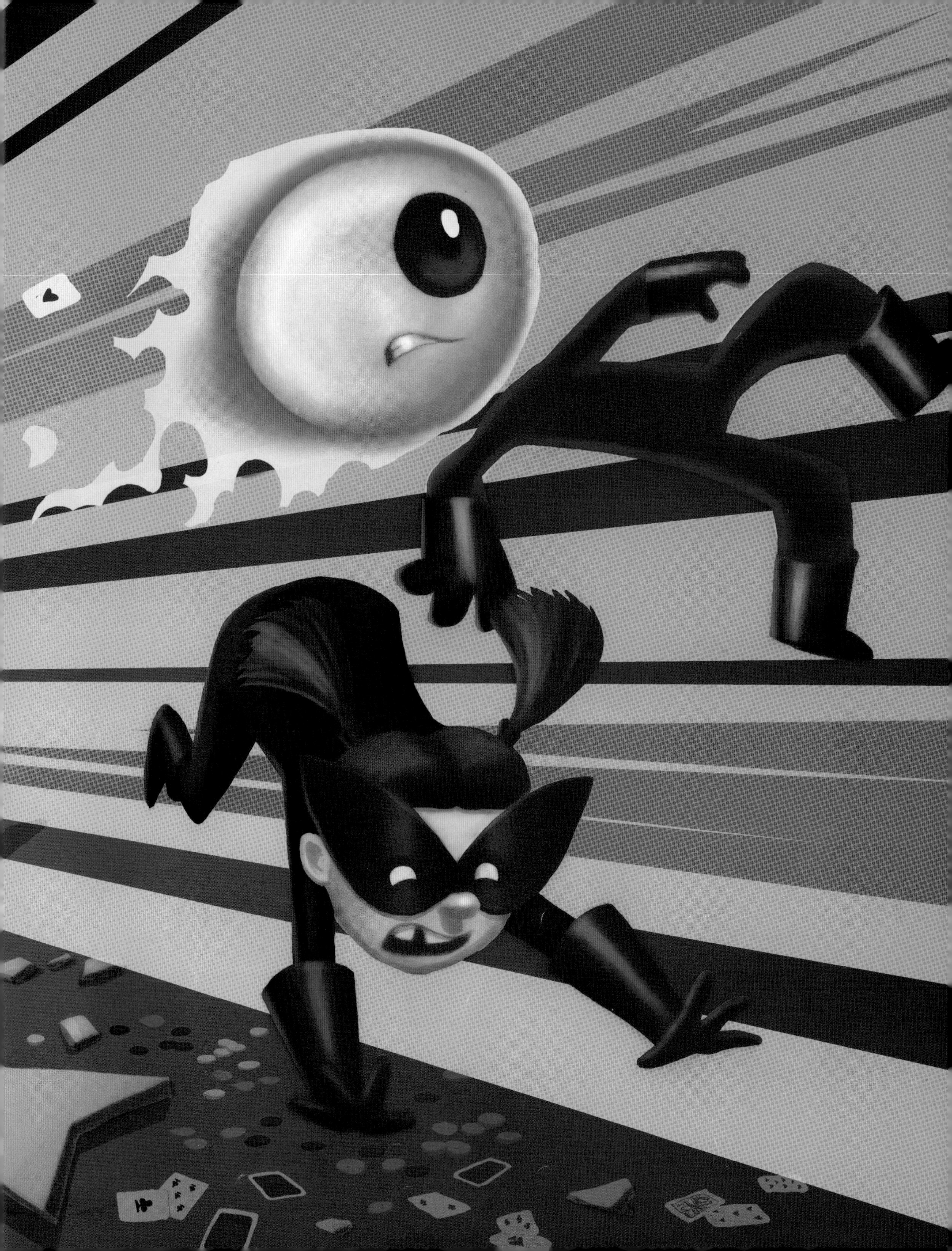

Then I make a quick
getaway back to the
Fortress of Awesome.

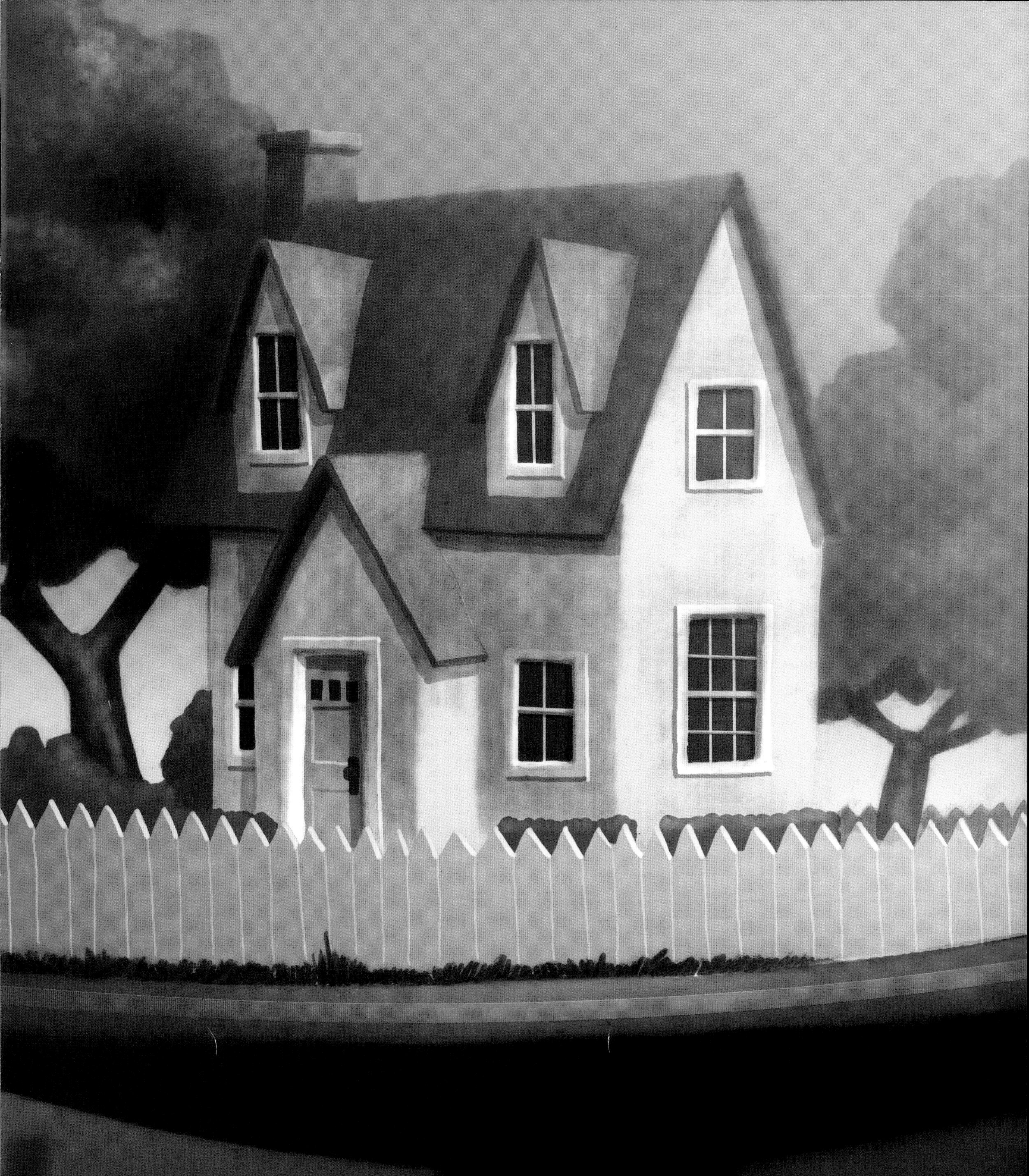

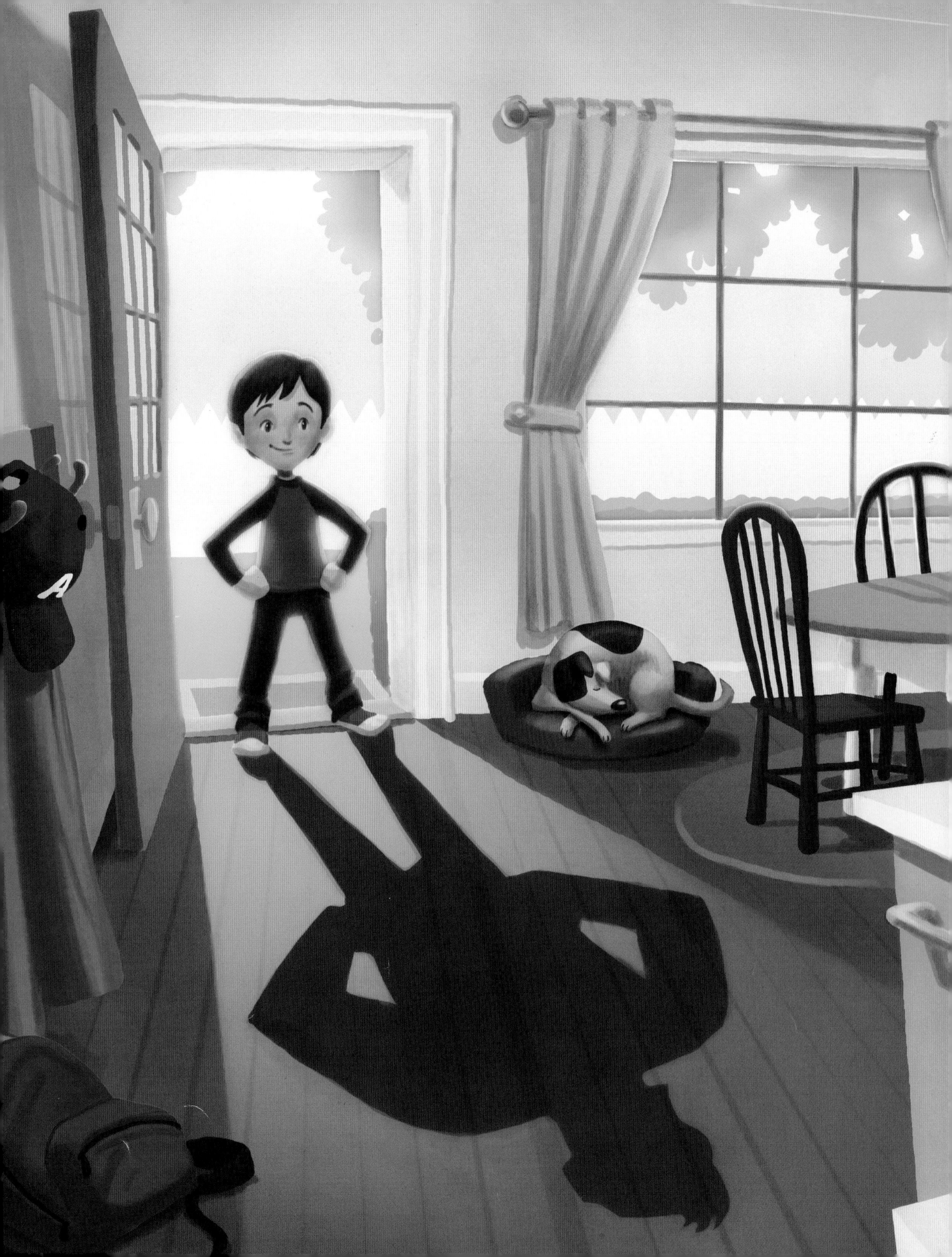

When I get there, my secret-identity mom is waiting for me, with a plate of plain old cheddar cheese and crackers, and chocolate milk. I'm so happy to see her, I throw a power grip around her, too.

She says that it feels AWESOME.

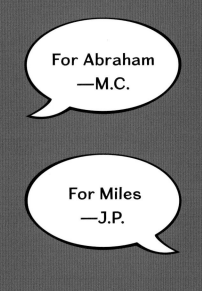

For Abraham
—M.C.

For Miles
—J.P.

Balzer + Bray is an imprint of HarperCollins Publishers.
Text and illustrations copyright © 2011 by Michael Chabon

Library of Congress Cataloging-in-Publication Data
Chabon, Michael.   The astonishing secret of Awesome Man / by Michael Chabon ;
illustrated by Jake Parker. — 1st ed.   p. cm.
Summary: A young superhero describes his awesome powers,
which he then demonstrates as various foes arrive on the scene.
ISBN 978-0-06-191462-1 (trade bdg.)
[1. Superheroes—Fiction. 2. Imagination—Fiction.
3. Family life—Fiction.] I. Parker, Jake, ill. II. Title.
PZ7.C3315Ast 2011   2010041192
[E]—dc22   CIP
AC

19 20 SCP   20 19 18 17 16 15 14 13
❖
First Edition

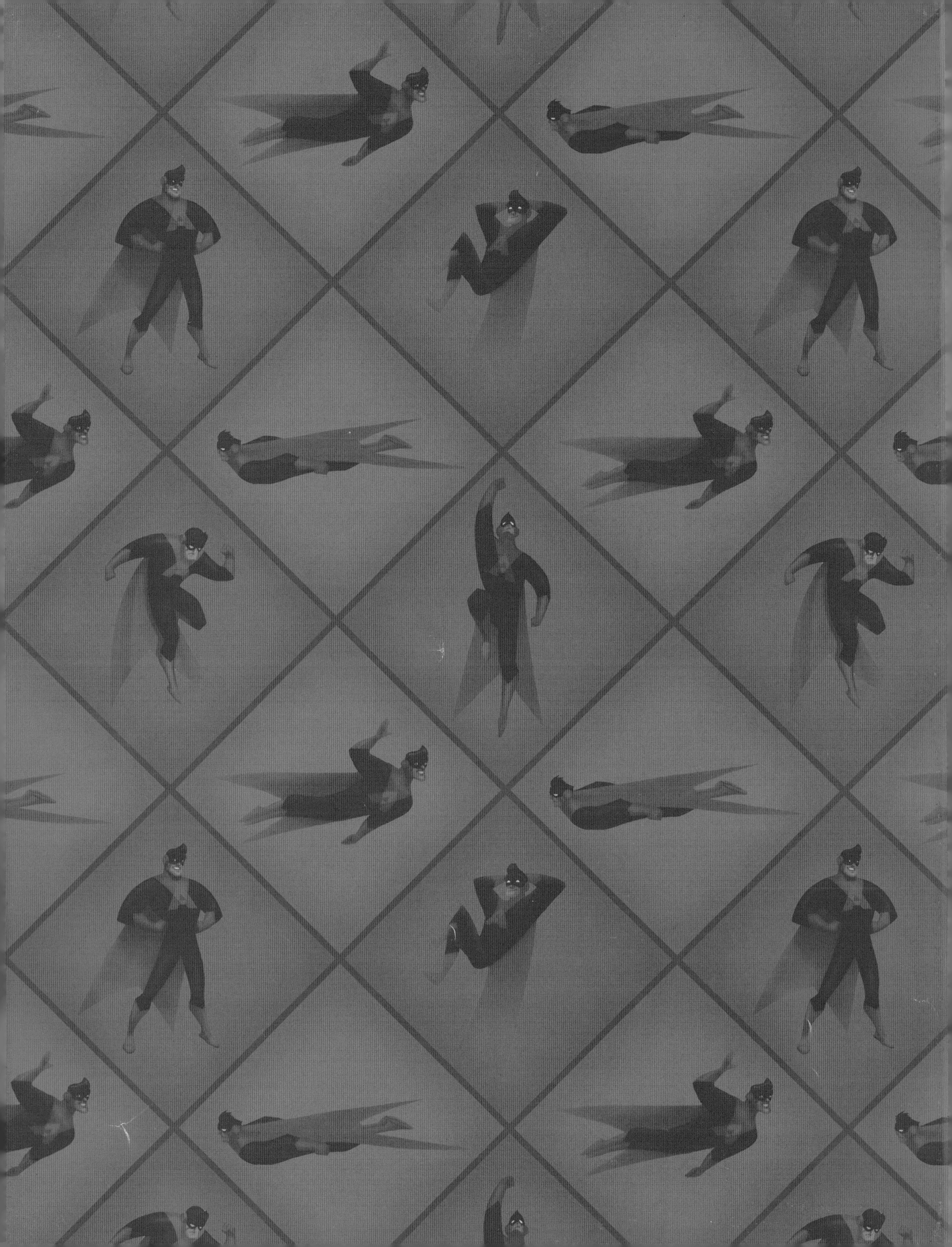